KEIKO KASZA

THE MIGHTIEST

G. P. Putnam's Sons
New York

G. P. Putnam's Sons, a division of Penguin Putnam Books for Young Readers,
345 Hudson Street, New York, NY 10014. G. P. Putnam's Sons, Reg. U.S. Pat. & Tm. Off.
Published simultaneously in Canada.
Printed in Hong Kong by South China Printing Co. (1988) Ltd.
Designed by Sharon Murray Jacobs.
Text set in 16.5-point Administer.
The art was done in gouache on three-ply Bristol illustration paper.
Library of Congress Cataloging-in-Publication Data
Kasza, Keiko.
The mightiest / Keiko Kasza. p. cm. Summary: The Lion, the Bear, and the Elephant
compete to see who can do the best job scaring a tiny old woman, but she has a surprise for
them. [1. Lions—Fiction. 2. Bears—Fiction. 3. Elephants—Fiction. 4. Giants—Fiction.] I. Title.
PZ7.K15645 Mi 2001 [E]—dc21 00-040296 ISBN 0-399-23586-8
10 9 8 7 6 5 4 3 2 1
First Impression

To Jamie and Danny

Deep in the quiet woods,
there was a golden crown sitting on a rock.

For the Mightiest

One day three animals discovered the crown.

"Finders, keepers!" yelled the Bear. "That's mine."

"No way," said the Elephant, "I saw it first."

"Wait, guys," said the Lion, "something is written there on the rock. It says, 'For the Mightiest.'"

For the Mightiest

"Well, then," said the Lion, grabbing the crown, "this is obviously mine."

"No, it's not," said the Bear, "I'm the mightiest."

"Step aside," said the Elephant, "and give me my crown."

On and on the animals argued. Suddenly, off in the distance, the Lion saw a tiny old woman walking toward them.

“Listen,” he whispered. “Let’s settle this once and for all. Each of us will try to scare that old lady. Whoever scares her the most wins the crown.”

“Sounds fair,” the others agreed.

So they hid behind the bushes and waited anxiously for the tiny old woman to come near. When she finally reached the bushes . . .

. . . the Lion jumped up.

"Rooarrrrr!"

"Oh, my!" cried the tiny old woman. "You scared the daylights out of me!"

Then the Bear jumped up.

"Grrrrrrrrrrrr!"

"Oh, my!" cried the tiny old woman. "You scared the daylights out of me!"

Finally, it was the Elephant's turn. He sucked in the air and . . .

"Baarrruuuu!"

"Oh, my!" cried the tiny old woman. "You scared the daylights out of me!"

There was no way of knowing who had scared the tiny old woman the most.

"My *roarrr* made her jump," boasted the Lion.

"My *grrrrr* had her shaking in her boots," growled the Bear.

"My *baarruuu* blew her away," shouted the Elephant.

They were so busy arguing, they didn't notice that they had company.

Suddenly, an enormous giant towered over them.

"Well, *roarrr-grrr-baarruu* on you!" he yelled. "I happen to be the biggest, the baddest, and the mightiest giant in the world. Now give me that crown."

With the crown on his head, the giant scooped up the three animals.

"To prove that I'm the mightiest," bellowed the giant, "I think I'll drop you off a cliff."

"Help! Someone, help us!" wailed the animals.

But who could help them now?

Just then, a high voice screeched . . .

. . . *"George!"*

The giant jumped in the air, dropped the three animals, and fell to the ground.

There, standing in front of the biggest, the baddest, and the mightiest giant in the world, was none other than . . . the tiny old woman.

She was scaring the daylights out of him!

"George!" she yelled. "How many times have I told you not to pick on poor, helpless creatures?"

"Umm, lots of times, Mama," whimpered the giant. "I won't do it again. Honest, Mama. I promise."

"Good, George," said the woman, "I'm glad to hear that."

The animals couldn't believe their eyes. They snatched the crown away from the giant . . .

. . . and presented it to the tiny old woman.

"Surely and positively," said the Lion.

"Without a doubt," said the Bear.

"This belongs to you, ma'am!" said the Elephant.

"Oh, my!" cried the tiny old woman. "How flattering!"

"But," said the woman, "I don't really need this. Let's put it back where you found it."

"Put it back?" they asked her.

"Yes," said the tiny old woman. "I have my little hat, and that's enough for me."

George and the animals looked at her with admiration.

The mightiest didn't need a crown after all!

As soon as they left, the woods became quiet again.
The golden crown sat peacefully on its rock, just like before.
But not for long . . .